THE
BEST TIME
OF DAY

THE
BEST
TIME
OF DAY

WRITTEN BY **Eileen Spinelli**

ILLUSTRATED BY **Bryan Langdo**

Gulliver Books
Harcourt, Inc.
Orlando   Austin   New York   San Diego   Toronto   London

Requests for permission to make copies of any part of the work should be mailed to the following address: Permissions Department, Harcourt, Inc., 6277 Sea Harbor Drive, Orlando, Florida 32887-6777.

www.HarcourtBooks.com

Gulliver Books is an imprint of Harcourt, Inc., registered in the United States of America and/or other jurisdictions.

Library of Congress Cataloging-in-Publication Data
Spinelli, Eileen.
The best time of day/Eileen Spinelli; illustrated by Bryan Langdo.
p.   cm.
"Gulliver Books."
Summary: Farmer Fred, various members of his family, and his neighbors each have a favorite time of day.
[1. Country life—Fiction.   2. Farm life—Fiction.   3. Day—Fiction.
4. Stories in rhyme.]   1. Langdo, Bryan, ill.   II. Title.
PZ8.3.S759Be   2005
[E]—dc22   2004005747
ISBN 0-15-205051-5

First edition
H G F E D C B A

Manufactured in China

The illustrations in this book were done in watercolor
on Fabriano Uno cold-press, 140 lb. paper.
The display lettering was created by Judythe Sieck.
The text type was set in Berling.
Color separations by Bright Arts Ltd., Hong Kong
Manufactured by South China Printing Company, Ltd., China
This book was printed on totally chlorine-free Stora Enso Matte paper.
Production supervision by Pascha Gerlinger
Designed by Lydia D'moch

For Doris Woodside . . . Martha Zerfoss . . .
Emily Hopkins . . . and Pat Broderick,
because one of the best times of day
is time spent with friends.
—E. S.

For Nikki,
any time I'm with you is my best time of day.
—B. L.

The best time of day for the rooster is when
the sun rises high over barnyard and pen.
He wakes up the farmer, the animals, too,
with his rowdy-dow "Cocka-doodle-dee-doo!"

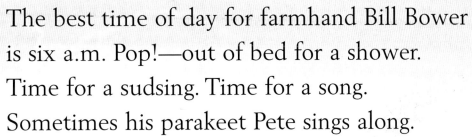

The best time of day for farmhand Bill Bower
is six a.m. Pop!—out of bed for a shower.
Time for a sudsing. Time for a song.
Sometimes his parakeet Pete sings along.

The best time of day for the farmer's wife, Mabel,
is breakfast—with pancakes and eggs on the table.
With apples a-sizzle and muffins galore,
and all of her family hungry for more.

The best time of day for the marmalade cat
is her midmorning nap in an old scarecrow hat.
Drowsy and cozy, she lets out a sigh—
and seems not to notice two mice scamper by.

The best time of day for the farmer's son, Joe,
is recess. The bell rings—he's ready to go.
The school yard backs up to a cornfield—what fun!
Let's play come-and-catch-me. How fast can you run?

The best time of day, declares Farmer Fred,
is eating his lunch in the shade of the shed—
with his dog alongside and a note from his wife:
"Kisses XXX—till supper." Ah, this is the life.

The best time of day for the neighbor Lynn Ives
is just after lunch, when the mail truck arrives
with postcards . . . or letters her granddaughter sends—
or a packet of snapshots from one of her friends.

The best time of day for baby Nicole
is two p.m.—onto the road for a stroll.
"Oink" to the piggies. *"Moo"* to the cow.
Wave hi to Daddy, who's riding the plow.

The best time of day for Joe's sister, Star,
is four—when she practices on the guitar.
Her music's so lovely (a warm bluesy style)
that Farmhand Bill stops to listen awhile.

The best time of day for Granny McCall
is five p.m. Why? That's when Gus comes to call.
The two of them sit on the porch swing together
and chat about chickens and changes in weather.

The best time of day for Granny's friend Gus
is when Mabel says, "Stay! Have supper with us.
There's plenty of corn bread and plenty of stew."
Gus sheepishly grins. "Don't mind if I do."

The farmer's dog finds that his best time of day
is dusk, when the spaniel down Mrs. Ives's way
starts barking—to Dog's ears it's more like a croon:
Come wander the meadow. Come wait for the moon.

Shh . . . Everyone's sleeping. The farm has grown still,
and nothing is stirring in starlight until
the barn owl awakens to softly take flight.
For Barn Owl the best time of day . . .

is the night.